Destination: Ooo

by Jake Black

illustrated by Shane L. Johnson

PSS!
PRICE STERN SLOAN
An Imprint of Penguin Group (USA) Inc.

PRICE STERN SLOAN
Published by the Penguin Group
Penguin Group (USA) Inc., 375 Hudson Street, New York, New York 10014, USA
Penguin Group (Canada), 90 Eglinton Avenue East, Suite 700,
Toronto, Ontario M4P 2Y3, Canada
(a division of Pearson Penguin Canada Inc.)
Penguin Books Ltd, 80 Strand, London WC2R 0RL, England
Penguin Ireland, 25 St Stephen's Green, Dublin 2, Ireland (a division of Penguin Books Ltd)
Penguin Group (Australia), 707 Collins Street, Melbourne, Victoria 3008, Australia
(a division of Pearson Australia Group Pty Ltd)
Penguin Books India Pvt Ltd, 11 Community Centre,
Panchsheel Park, New Delhi — 110 017, India
Penguin Group (NZ), 67 Apollo Drive, Rosedale, Auckland 0632,
New Zealand (a division of Pearson New Zealand Ltd)
Penguin Books (South Africa), Rosebank Office Park,
181 Jan Smuts Avenue, Parktown North 2193, South Africa
Penguin China, B7 Jiaming Center, 27 East Third Ring Road North,
Chaoyang District, Beijing 100020, China

Penguin Books Ltd, Registered Offices: 80 Strand, London WC2R 0RL, England

Published in 2013 by Price Stern Sloan, a division of Penguin Young Readers
Group, 345 Hudson Street, New York, New York 10014. PSS! is a registered
trademark of Penguin Group (USA) Inc. Printed in the U.S.A.

ISBN 978-0-8431-7328-4   10 9 8 7 6 5 4 3 2 1

ALWAYS LEARNING   **PEARSON**

Introduction

Oh my glob, you've decided to visit the Land of Ooo. Do you really think that's a good idea? You know it's, like, superdangerous and kind of crazy there, right? Oh. You do. Okay, well then, off we go! This book was specially created to help you spot the coolest, most awesome sites in all of Ooo, from the Candy Kingdom, to Parallel Dimensions, to the scary Underworld! We'll tell you what to look for, what to stay away from, what to eat, the famous residents, and even some totally unboring history.

Make sure you carry this book with you at all times (it makes a totally kick-butt weapon).

Contents

4

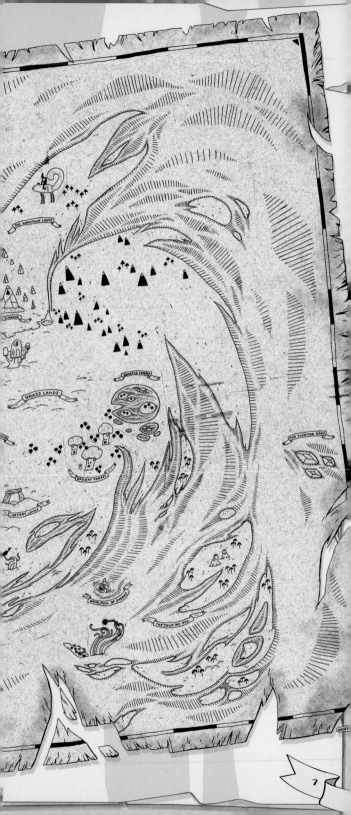

THE UNKNOWN LANDS

KINGDOM

GRASS LANDS

HAUNTED SWAMP

SPOOKY FOREST

THE FLOATING GEMS

DESERT LANDS

WHIRLPOOL OF TERROR

THE SQUID INK SEA

GROFF

7

Finn and Jake's Tree Fort

Our first stop is the house belonging to adventurers Jake and Finn. It's a tree fort. Actually it's a whole tree. The trunk is hollow — that's where Jake and Finn keep all their scores of gold and jewels and junk from their adventures.

They have a Weapons Room where they store their weapons. What did you think it held? Lollipops?

The bedroom is always a mess. It's where their beds are. They can get there by climbing a ladder. They like to sleep in it after a hard day's work adventuring.

In the Tree Fort's living room, Jake and Finn unwind. They play video games with their roommate, BMO, and watch movies. It's decorated with pictures of Jake and Finn having adventures together.

Finn

One of the main residents of the Tree Fort is Finn. A human warrior, Finn is known throughout the Land of Ooo as one of its greatest adventurers and heroes. He is very brave (most of the time) and loves to rush into danger. Sometimes he doesn't think things through before he dives into action, but that's why we love him.

He loves to fight bad guys and rescue girls in peril.

Everybody knows his crush
is Princess Bubblegum of
the Candy Kingdom, but
he doesn't know that everybody
knows. And that's okay.

If you ever see Finn coming to
your rescue, you can know that the best
hero of the Land of Ooo will save your day!

Jake

A cool, calm, collected dog, Jake likes living in the Tree Fort. He likes pretty much everything about it. I mean, c'mon, what dog wouldn't like having a tree that everyone knows is his! He's a popular warrior, too. With powers beyond those of a normal dog — like the ability to stretch, twist, and contort his body — he has become as much a hero in the Land of Ooo as his buddy Finn. Jake also loves the ladies, or at least one lady. Lady Rainicorn, that is. You can catch Jake hanging out with Lady

Rainicorn and his best friend, Finn, at the Tree Fort kind of a lot. Also, he loves video games.

BMO

Another well-known resident of the wacky Tree Fort is BMO, or as Jake and Finn call it, "BMO." BMO is a video game unit. Games can be played on it as a handheld gaming device or using the two controllers that come out of its screen. One of BMO's coolest features is a secret button that, once pushed, lets users play video games inside BMO's main-braingame-frame. The players get turned into video-game versions of themselves and play the game for real!

Besides video games, BMO likes to play non-video-game games with its

roommates. Games like cards, sports, and hide-and-seek (okay, we haven't confirmed that last one, but you get the idea). Finn and Jake love that they have a game unit for a roommate.

Language

As with most of the Land of Ooo, English is the primary language of the Tree Fort. Though Finn and Jake know each other so well, you'd think they would have their own secret language. They don't. They do, however, speak using the slang terms and language of their culture. These words include:

🔆 Awesome!

🔆 Showzow!

🔆 Slamacow!

🔆 Mathematical!

🔆 Algebraic!

🔆 Righteous!

🔆 Wrongeous!

🔆 Rhombus!

🔆 Radical!

🔆 Dude!

Food

You'd think that in a place where all the people, buildings, and everything are made from candy, the food would be all about candy. But it's not. Not even a little. In the Tree Fort kitchen, you'll find some delicious noncandy edibles like:

- ❋ **Ice Cream Pizza:** scoops of ice cream sandwiched between two slices of pizza

- Softy Cheese: a soft, almost saucy, cheese that is sold in a can or from a squirter in convenience stores

- Everything Burrito: A masterpiece of culinary excellence, the Everything Burrito is a massive burrito invented by Jake that includes everything edible in the world, and then a little bit more that you might not ever think to eat

Landmarks

When visiting the Tree Fort, be sure to visit the following landmarks and get your picture taken at them:

- ❁ The Living Room clock with an inscription that reads FINN AND JAKE: TIMELESS

- ❁ The bathroom, because everyone should visit the bathroom before they leave

- Finn's bed, with its pelts and skins of various types

- The hollow tree trunk, just because

- The artwork in the Living Room, because it's one of a kind and a masterpiece

- The well outside, because it's a passage to another dimension

Important/Historical Events

Lots of interesting things have happened in the Tree Fort:

- ⚙ Vampire Queen Marceline used to live in it, before Finn and Jake.

- ⚙ When the video game Guardians of Sunshine came to life, the Tree Fort's hollow tree trunk exploded.

- The Tree Fort was basically destroyed and rebuilt after it was attacked by a love-stricken Snorlock.

- It is the base of operations for Finn and Jake before they go on any adventure. As such, almost all of the historical and significant events in the modern history of the Land of Ooo have their beginnings in the Tree Fort.

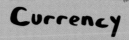

When visiting a foreign land, it is good to know what kind of currency, or money, the natives use. In the Land of Ooo, the currency is a lot like the money in the world you're used to living in. It's dollar bills. The only difference is that they are either small or giant. Small dollars are used by regular-size people, and giant dollars are used by giants.

A lot of folks in the Land of Ooo just avoid the money situation altogether and choose to trade goods and services with each other.

Other people like to use gold and jewels to buy stuff. These can also be used to pay taxes. And to be stored in your Tree Fort as prizes from adventures you go on.

Candy Kingdom

A place made entirely out of candy? It must be every kid's dream! (It is.) It must be the happiest place in the universe! (It's that, too.) There must be superhappy, fun parties all the time! (There are.) The Candy Kingdom is exactly what it sounds like. Ruled by the beautiful Princess Bubblegum, the Candy Kingdom is home to some of the greatest people and places in all the Land of Ooo.

Many adventures take place here in the Candy Kingdom. And why not? It's such a great place to visit, of course everyone wants to go there. Good guys love living there. Bad guys love trying to conquer it. And candy is delicious.

Bubblegum Castle

At the center of the Candy Kingdom is Bubblegum Castle. There, Princess Bubblegum rules over her people with an iron fist. Okay, not even close. Probably more like a taffy palm. And a smile. Like everything in the Candy Kingdom, Bubblegum Castle is made out of candy, ice cream, and everything delicious.

Like every castle, it's got moats, drawbridges, and high towers. It's got a dungeon, but even that's not too scary—after all, it's made out of candy. If visiting the Land of Ooo and the Candy Kingdom, Bubblegum Castle is a must-see. And a must-eat. You probably shouldn't eat the castle itself, but try some of the food made by the castle's incredible cooking staff.

Princess Bubblegum

Perhaps there is no one more sugary sweet (see what I did there?) in all the Land of Ooo than Princess Bonnibel Bubblegum. She is the happiest, most beautiful person in all the land, and she rules over the Candy People with incredible kindness and goodness. She loves the color pink and likes performing scientific experiments. Her subjects, the Candy People, love her completely.

Being a teenager, she is still young enough to have fun, but old enough to have adventures protecting and defending her people. Finn was completely in love with her. While the princess liked Finn as a friend, though, she was not attached to any suitor at that time. Everything she does is for the good of her people.

Candy People

The Candy People are exactly what they sound like they'd be: people made out of candy and other sweet foods (like fruits). There are several prominent citizens in the Candy Kingdom, such as:

- Candy Cane Man
- Banana Popsicle
- Earl of Lemongrab
- Cinnamon Bun
- Jelly Bean

- 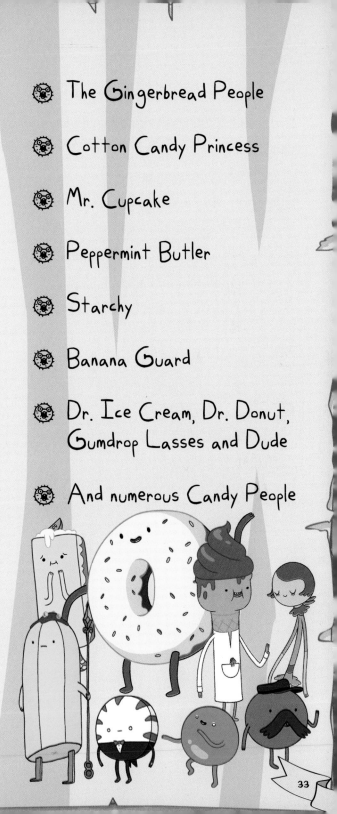 The Gingerbread People
- Cotton Candy Princess
- Mr. Cupcake
- Peppermint Butler
- Starchy
- Banana Guard
- Dr. Ice Cream, Dr. Donut, Gumdrop Lasses and Dude
- And numerous Candy People

Military

In order to protect itself from the surrounding enemy kingdoms, the Candy Kingdom has a small-but-powerful military force known as the Gumball Guardians. No one knows the structure of the Candy Kingdom's armed forces, but Jake and Finn have seen many advanced weapons made out of candy, including candy helicopters. Fortunately, the Candy Kingdom hasn't had to use these candy weapons in very many battles.

On a more local level, the Candy Kingdom is protected by a group of protectors known as the Banana Guard. These banana-looking people stand guard around the castle, protecting Princess Bubblegum and making sure no one in the kingdom gets hurt or anything. Like the princess and kingdom they protect, they are very happy—surprisingly so for cops.

Candy Tavern and Mental Hospital

Every town, every city, and every kingdom has a "bad part of town." Sometimes it's called "the wrong side of the tracks." In the Bubblegum Kingdom, that bad part of town is the Candy Tavern. The angriest, meanest, evilest Candy People can be found in there. Folks like Jaybird and his gang hang out there. Apple thieves, candy vandals, and other scum are found in this wretched tavern.

The mental hospital is also a less-than-sweet place to visit in the Candy Kingdom, but unlike the tavern, its occupants are nice people, even if they're crazy. It also houses some of the Candy Kingdom's oldest citizens, helping them find happiness in their later years.

When visiting the Candy Kingdom, these are the most important places to visit:

- The Candy Castle: It's the most famous monument in the entire kingdom.

- Lemongrab: It's an additional territory ruled over by the kingdom.

- Duchy of Nuts: It's another territory ruled over by the kingdom.

- The Church: It's a mysterious religious center hardly anyone has ever seen.

- The Noncandy Areas, including Finn and Jake's Tree Fort: There are areas surrounding the kingdom that are not made of candy. These are a must-see since they are rare exceptions in the Candy Kingdom.

Important/ Historical Events

Almost every adventure and exciting experience that happens in the Land of Ooo happens in the Candy Kingdom. Some events to pay particular notice to are:

- ◉ When the kingdom fought off invasions from the Marshmallow kids, the Hyooman tribe, Magic Penguins, and some wolves

- ◉ There was one time when a black hole opened and almost swallowed the kingdom.

- The kingdom has faced knife storms.

- Many, many parties—like science barbecues and birthday parties

- An attempted coup from the Earl of Lemongrab, who tried to seize Princess Bubblegum's throne

- A zombie apocalypse

- When Princess Bubblegum created a temporary immortal replacement

Crystal Dimension

In another magical dimension, weird stuff happens. It's a dimension filled with pink crystals. Crystal everything: crystal walls, crystal people, even crystal food. Weird, right? There are a couple ways to get to the crystal dimension. You can bite a special crystal gem apple. You can enter through a portal between the dimensions. A lot of crystals will open these portals. But you better be sure you want to go there. The Crystal Dimension is a place of mystery. It's a place of magic. It's a place where war once ravaged the entire dimension. Only a few people from the normal dimension have gone there. Finn is one of them. He found a crystal that opened a portal on his doorstep, and then he had some adventures on the other side.

Rainicorns

Many of the mysteries of the Crystal Dimension concern its inhabitants. It is believed that rainicorns are some of the residents in the strange pink dimension. These creatures have long bodies striped with the colors of the rainbow. (It's notable that one color is missing from their bodies: orange.) As with the Crystal Dimension itself, not much is known about these creatures beyond their ability to fly and their power to change the color of an object by blasting it with their horns.

How prevalent rainicorns are in the Crystal Dimension is unknown, but it is a known fact that some live there. They got their land as the result of victory in war.

Lady Rainicorn and Family

The only rainicorns from the Crystal Dimension that anyone in Ooo knows about for sure are Lady Rainicorn and her family. Lady Rainicorn is Jake's girlfriend. The two care about each other a lot. Jake was probably never more nervous than when he was about to meet Lady Rainicorn's parents, Bob and Ethel. It has been long known that the wars in the Crystal Dimension were between dogs and rainicorns. Bob and Ethel like Jake, though, because a dog once saved Bob's life.

Bob and Ethel live at 47 Rainbow Street in the Crystal Dimension. They both wear glasses. Not every rainicorn wears glasses, but Bob and Ethel do because of poor vision. They also use Universal Translators when they visit the Candy Kingdom.

Language (Korean)

The number of languages spoken in the Crystal Dimension is unknown. It is known, however, that rainicorns speak Korean. They are the only species known to speak it. When traveling to the Crystal Dimension, a Universal Translator will help you communicate with those who speak Korean. Furthermore, the translator will help them understand you if you don't speak Korean.

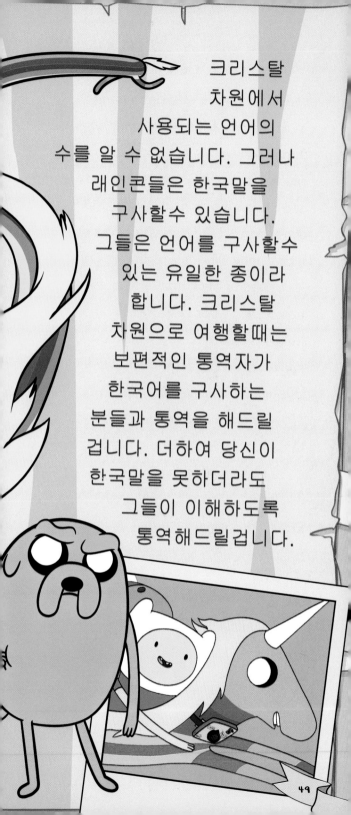

크리스탈
차원에서
사용되는 언어의
수를 알 수 없습니다. 그러나
래인콘들은 한국말을
구사할수 있습니다.
그들은 언어를 구사할수
있는 유일한 종이라
합니다. 크리스탈
차원으로 여행할때는
보편적인 통역자가
한국어를 구사하는
분들과 통역을 해드릴
겁니다. 더하여 당신이
한국말을 못하더라도
그들이 이해하도록
통역해드릴겁니다.

Rainicorn-Dog War

For thousands of years, the Crystal Dimension was caught in an epic war. It was a struggle between the dogs and the rainicorns that inhabit the dimension. There may have been other factions involved, too. A drawing of the war, done by Jake, implies that flying saucers and laser guns were among the weapons of choice. It is believed that the rainicorns won the war, because they still live in the Crystal Dimension.

The war has resulted in heated tension between dogs and rainicorns. Bob Rainicorn, however, is an exception. An unnamed dog saved Bob's life during the war. The dog was captured, but Bob never forgot the noble act during the millennia-long war.

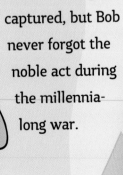

Food (Crystal Dimension Apples; Humans)

In a dimension made entirely out of crystals, it makes sense to wonder what the people who live there eat. There are, once again, no simple answers. They do eat. But we're not 100 percent sure *what* they eat.

We know there are crystal gem apples. They seem to be powerful and might even be held sacred by the people of the Crystal Dimension. Crystal gem apples are protected by the Crystal

Guardians. Biting one can take you from the Candy Kingdom to the Crystal Dimension. Apples such as this also seem to be extremely rare. In fact, Tree Trunks is the only creature not from the Crystal Dimension known to have bitten into one.

There is also a common and consistent rumor that rainicorns eat humans. This is unsubstantiated, but if a human travels to the Crystal Dimension, it's recommended that they keep their guard up and not get eaten.

Crystal Guardians

It is believed that, in addition to dogs and rainicorns, the primary residents of the Crystal Dimension are the Crystal Guardians. Their function is a little unclear. We know that they protect the crystal gem apples so creatures from the Candy Kingdom don't bite into one and enter the Crystal Dimension. They've also been seen doing the bidding of the rulers of the Crystal Dimension. The Guardians have limited speaking ability—mostly they repeat what they hear. They can transform creatures into crystal beings.

It is not known how many Crystal Guardians exist. They may be a vast army or, more likely, a small security force protecting the upper class and the precious valuables of the Crystal Dimension. Approach with caution!

Important/ Historical Events

Some of the most important things to happen in the Crystal Dimension (that we know about, at least) are these:

- The Rainicorn-Dog War

- The time Tree Trunks bit a crystal gem apple and went to the dimension for the first time

- 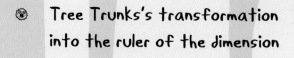 Tree Trunks's transformation into the ruler of the dimension

- Finn's abduction and escape from the dimension

Ice Kingdom

If the Candy Kingdom is the warmest, happiest place in the world, then the Ice Kingdom is its polar opposite. It's cold. It's scary. It's unpleasant. And above all, it's really, really, totally, completely evil.

It's so unpleasant that it's sparsely populated. Not many people or creatures want to live there. Too cold. Those who do live there are mostly made of ice and snow. As its name suggests, the Ice Kingdom is a frozen land ruled by the wicked Ice King.

It's not welcoming to visitors. In fact, one of the Ice Kingdom's laws is "no trespassing." There are other very complicated laws in the land. (See page 66 for an in-depth explanation of these laws. Sort of. As much as we can figure them out . . .)

Ice King

The Ice Kingdom is ruled by the Ice King, a coldhearted thousand-year-old dictator whose favorite pastime is kidnapping princesses from surrounding kingdoms and trying to marry them. He never succeeds, though.

He wears a powerful crown that gives him magic abilities, including the power of flight.

The crown also has
made him insane and
even altered his physical
appearance, down to his beard
and cold, blue skin.

He was once a human known as
Simon Petrikov. But then he discovered
his crown and became the Ice King.

His subjects in the Ice Kingdom
don't like him very much, but
that's okay with him because
he doesn't like them very
much, either.

His archenemies
are Jake and Finn, who
always stop his sinister
schemes.

Ice King's Castle

In the center of the Ice Kingdom is the Ice King's Castle. It's the only known structure in the kingdom. It's a giant, hollowed-out mountain covered in snow and ice. It's extremely cold and unwelcoming. It's impossible to climb because of the slippery ice that covers its exterior.

The entrance looks like a face. Inside, the Ice King has a living room, kitchen, bedroom (with giant bed), and other normal rooms inside a home. The Ice King apparently does not have a cleaning staff. His home is a mess. A big mess.

Visitors are not welcome at the castle. There are strict "no trespassing" laws in place throughout the Ice Kingdom, especially at the castle.

Landmarks

If you visit the Ice Kingdom (which is not recommended for travelers because of the Ice King's no trespassing laws, and also because it's freezing!) these are some sites to make sure you check out:

- 🅾 The Ice King's Castle (front)

- 🅾 The Ice King's Castle (back)

- 🅾 The Ice King's Castle (entrance)

- 🅾 The Ice King's Castle (top)

- 🅾 The Ice King's Castle is pretty much the only place to go when visiting the Ice Kingdom.

- 🅾 Wait! There's also the Snow Golem's cabin, adjacent to the castle.

Ice Kingdom Law and Marriages

The Ice King desperately wants to marry a princess from a neighboring kingdom. He doesn't really care which princess or which kingdom. He often kidnaps princesses to achieve this. Most of the time, Princess Bubblegum is his target.

As part of his marriage efforts, the Ice King has created elaborate laws and rules that travelers to the kingdom must be aware of. Apparently, all marriages require the bride be tied up and touch the groom's beard. The bride is also lowered from the ceiling by ropes. The ropes, according to Ice Kingdom tradition and law, bring good luck.

Legal experts in the Candy Kingdom are skeptical of the laws' and traditions' validity. They believe they were simply created to help the Ice King kidnap princesses. Travelers should be aware of these laws prior to visiting, however.

Important/ Historical Events

Some of the most important events in the Ice Kingdom's history are:

- ❄ When Jake and Finn freed a group of princesses from being married to the Ice King

- ❄ The Ice King's Manlorette Party was epic.

- ❄ When the Ice King left to help one of his friends, and Jake and Finn didn't believe he would actually help anyone

- ❄ The Ice King once froze Jake and Finn together to force them to become better friends.

- ❄ The great Wizard Battle, when Finn entered to stop the Ice King from winning

Ricardio

Ricardio's full name is Ricardio the Heart Man. He is literally the heart of the Ice King. The Ice King is so evil that he lost his need for a heart. Following a failed experiment, Ricardio set out for life on his own away from the king. Like the Ice King, Ricardio wants the heart of Princess Bubblegum, though unlike with the Ice King, this desire is literal

and not romantic. And like the Ice King, he's been stopped in his quest by Finn and Jake. He's even been defeated by Princess Bubblegum herself.

In the past, he fashioned himself a body out of another person's limbs. They gave him better mobility, but made him seem like more of a monster than a "heart."

Aside from the Ice King and Ricardio, the Ice Kingdom has some unique residents, many (if not most) of whom were created by the Ice King's magic. These include:

Lumpy Space Kingdom

Have you ever wanted to visit a castle in a cloud? Go to a city in outer space? Use a secret password to travel through a frog's innards? Then the Lumpy Space Kingdom is the right place for you. Home of the Lumpy Space People, the Lumpy Space Kingdom is a city that exists in outer space.

Be warned, though, that in the Lumpy Space Kingdom the residents don't like non-Lumpy people very much. They call them "smoothies." Like werewolves, they can turn you into a Lumpy Person if they bite you. On the other hand, it's pretty cool. I mean, it's a kingdom in space that's a city, with lumpy, cloudlike people!

Lumpy Space Princess

The Lumpy Space Kingdom is ruled over by the Lumpy Space Royal Family. The most famous member of the royal family is the Lumpy Space Princess. However, unlike many other princesses in the Land of Ooo, the Lumpy Space Princess is not the ruler of her kingdom. Her parents rule. In fact, the Lumpy Space Princess has been exiled to the dark reaches of the Candy Kingdom. There she terrorized a village.

She's not very nice and, like all Lumpy Space People, can infect people with "lumps" if she bites them. She has battled Finn and Jake many times, even biting them on occasion. But she always loses to them, and she hates that.

Entering the Lumpy Space Kingdom (Frog)

Most kingdoms are accessible by simply going there. You might have to go through the woods or hitch a ride or hike or something. But the Lumpy Space Kingdom is totally different. And totally gross. If you want to get there, simply go to the Cotton Candy Forest and search for a frog. The mysterious frog sits on a toadstool. If you give him the secret

password, which our sources have determined to be "Whatevers 2009," you'll be magically transported through the frog to the Lumpy Space Kingdom. Gross, right?

There are apparently other entrances to the kingdom, but we're not sure where or how to get there through them. So you gotta find the frog.

Lumpy Language

The Lumpy Space People have their own unique language. These are some terms you need to know if you visit the Lumpy Space Kingdom:

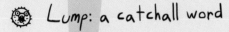 *Smoothies*: non-Lumpy people

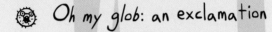 *Lump*: a catchall word

Oh my glob: an exclamation

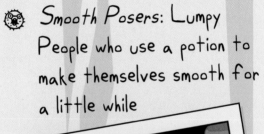 *Smooth Posers*: Lumpy People who use a potion to make themselves smooth for a little while

Smoothies

"Smoothies" is the derogatory term used by the Lumpy People for people who do not have the same cloudlike shape they have. This applies to humans, dogs, rainicorns, and every type of species that may visit the Lumpy Space Kingdom. Smoothies are considered second-class citizens there. Some Lumpy People sometimes try to experiment with living as a smoothie by taking an antidote that makes them appear human. These are called Smooth Posers, however, and they are not popular in the mainstream culture of the kingdom.

If a Lumpy Person bites a smoothie, he or she can turn that individual into a Lumpy Person in the same way a vampire or werewolf attacks and changes its victims. Don't let a Lumpy Person chomp down on you.

Landmarks

There are a few landmarks to make sure you see on your visit to the Lumpy Space Kingdom:

- **Make-Out Point:** a high point overlooking the kingdom where the Lumpy People go to kiss a lot

- **Lumpy Space School:** exactly what it sounds like

- **Lumpy Space Princess's house:** the residence of the Lumpy Space Princess before she was exiled

- **Lumpy Space Event Saloon:** where the city's events take place

- **Lumpy Abyss:** see section about this on page 88

Important/ Historical Events

There are a few big events that have taken place in the Lumpy Space Kingdom:

- Promcoming Dance: the annual dance where the Lumpy Space People relax and have fun with each other

- The time when the king and queen of the Lumpy Space Kingdom asked Jake and Finn to find the princess and bring her home

- When Lumpy Space Princess wrote her tell-all memoir and spied on Finn and Jake

Lumpy Abyss

The Lumpy Space Kingdom is made up of several lumpy masses where the people live. Between the masses, though, is the Lumpy Abyss. It's a bottomless pit that can suck people into oblivion if they aren't careful. The Lumpy Space People, and you if you travel there, use flying cars to move from place to place and avoid being sucked into the abyss.

Finn and Jake are familiar with the Lumpy Space Abyss, having seen it up close on their trips to the Lumpy Space Kingdom. Fortunately, because Finn was bit and became a little Lumpy, he can float over the Abyss. This has let him save Jake from certain doom in the pit.

Fire Kingdom

Volcanoes. Seas of lava. Heat. If that's what you're seeing and feeling, you must have entered the Fire Kingdom. All of the heat and fire elements in the Land of Ooo are found there. The Fire Kingdom is known as being the most evil place in all the Land of Ooo. Its people hate everyone else with the burning passion of a thousand suns.

This travel guide wouldn't be doing its job if it didn't advise against visiting this area. We will provide information for you on the following pages if you must visit there, but we cannot emphasize enough: DO NOT VISIT THIS KINGDOM. It's on fire. You will get burned. Or at least sweat a TON.

Fire Monarchy/ Flame King

The leader of the Fire Kingdom is the Flame King, the evil heir of the Fire Monarchy. He is protective of his evil daughter, the Flame Princess (having locked her in a lantern from time to time to protect her). The Flame King doesn't hesitate to execute people who anger him, and is known for having a hot temper. He is a very hot body—literally.

The Flame King is the largest of the Fire People, and wears a suit of armor to protect himself. He became the king after extinguishing his brother, one of his most evil acts. He loves being king. He makes it a point to remind everyone of his kingliness and power.

Fire Palace

The Fire Palace is a home fit for
a king—a king made of fire! The Fire
Palace features a giant throne room
where the Flame King sits on a fiery,
red-hot throne. His subjects, the little
Flame People, surround him, sitting on
stairs and wherever else they can be.
Above the throne hangs a lantern where
the Flame King has trapped his daughter
the Flame Princess.

From his throne, the Flame King issues his evil orders and makes his evil demands. His subjects carry them out. Finn and Jake have confronted the king in his palace and were lucky to escape with their lives.

If you can't stand the heat, get out of the palace!

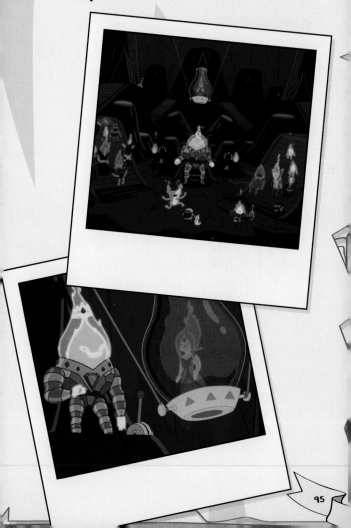

Some of the most frightening creatures in the Fire Kingdom are the Fire Wolves. These animals are vicious and attack their enemies, the snow creatures of the Ice Kingdom. The wolves are black with red streaks flowing through their bodies. They appear to be made of volcanic rocks with lava "blood veins." They have yellow-orange eyes, and they get angry over the littlest things. When angry, they turn into balls of fire. This makes them more dangerous than your average animal in the Land of Ooo.

If you encounter a Fire Wolf, the proper procedure is to not make eye contact, back away slowly and, above all, for the love of all that is good and candy, do NOT make a face like a snowman!

Landmarks

In the Fire Kingdom, there are several significant sites—but . . . DO NOT GO THERE!

- The Fire Palace: the center of the government of the Flame Kingdom—DO NOT GO THERE!

- Sea of Flames: the lava that surrounds the kingdom—DO NOT GO THERE!

- Isle of Steam: a waterway that borders the Fire Kingdom, but is always evaporating because of the kingdom's heat—DO NOT GO THERE!

Border with the Ice Kingdom

PLAYER SELECT

FIRE KING

The Fire Kingdom has an enemy in the Ice Kingdom. It is believed that the Ice Kingdom and the Fire Kingdom either border each other or are at least very, very close. Both kingdoms are known throughout the Land of Ooo to be inhabited by mean creatures and led by evil kings. When the two elements collide, it can get really melty for the ice

ICE KING

creatures — and then the fire creatures
can be extinguished by the watery,
melted ice creatures.

It's unknown if the Isle of Steam is
part of the Ice Kingdom or just water.
Regardless, the warring factions of the
Ice and Fire Kingdoms are just another
reason for us to say DO NOT GO THERE.

Important/ Historical Events

Some crazy stuff has happened in the Fire Kingdom, like:

* The time the adventurers had to save the Cotton Candy Princess from the Fire Count

* When Jake and Finn tried to meet and hook up with the Flame Princess, and she turned out to be evil and mean

* The time that Finn and Jake snuck into the Fire Kingdom to get the Flame Princess's candles back

* Jake, Finn, and Lady Rainicorn had a picnic near the Fire Kingdom once, too.

Flame Princess

A daddy's girl she is not. The Flame
Princess is the daughter of the Flame
King. And to say they don't get along is
putting it mildly. And there's nothing
mild about anything in the Fire Kingdom
or this family. The Flame King
is so protective of his daughter
that he's held her captive in
a lantern that hangs over
his throne.

She has escaped and moved out of her father's house to live in the Candy Kingdom. She and Finn have had an on-again, off-again romantic relationship. The Flame Princess is intense. She has been called evil (by her father) and passionate (by Finn). Regardless of her true nature and feelings, she makes life exciting one way or another for the people that know her.

Mushroom War

The Land of Ooo is a strange place. It's been called a "postapocalyptic wasteland." No one really knows why it is the way it is, with its strange and magical kingdoms and creatures. One thing that is known, though, is that it all was caused by the Mushroom War.

Not much is known about the Mushroom War itself, except that two people survived: the Ice King and Marceline. Even they, though, don't remember or talk about the war, except to say a "mushroom bomb" was dropped on the world one thousand years ago.

The war caused a chunk of planet Earth to be blown off, and resulted in the creation of the new Land of Ooo.

Marceline's House and the Nightosphere

Vampire Queen Marceline lives in the most unlikely of homes. It looks like a normal house from before the Mushroom War. It's pink (a weird color for a vampire's house), and it has a basketball hoop and even a white picket fence. Maybe the only thing about the house that seems vampire-y is that it's in a dark cave.

But really, what's vampire-y?
Vampires really can live anywhere.
Maybe it's not so surprising because
Marceline is, of course, a teenage girl.
Sort of. Anyway, she likes living there,
even if it seems like a weird place for her
to live. Marceline is pretty much always
different than anyone expects her to be.

Marceline

Marceline is a thousand-year-old vampire. She plays rock music with her vicious-looking guitars. When she first met Finn and Jake, she was an enemy, but they've become very good friends. Now she's one of their closest allies.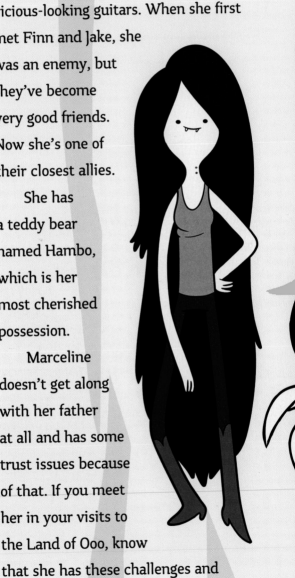

She has a teddy bear named Hambo, which is her most cherished possession.

Marceline doesn't get along with her father at all and has some trust issues because of that. If you meet her in your visits to the Land of Ooo, know that she has these challenges and that anything mean she says to you isn't personal.

As a vampire, Marceline has many mysterious powers, such as shape-shifting and flying.

Zombie Poodle

Another resident of Marceline's happy home is Schwabl. Fluffy and white, Schwabl looks like your average poodle. But the reality is that Schwabl is actually an undead dog called a zombie poodle. It's not known how Schwabl came into being after dying. It is presumed that Marceline brought him back to life using some of her vampire powers.

Marceline doesn't have a lot of companionship in her life, but Schwabl fills some of that need. Marceline installed a dog door into her house for Schwabl to get in and out of her house.

Schwabl is not your typical house dog. He doesn't bark or attack visitors. He will follow them around the house, as he's done with Finn and Jake. Ultimately, Schwabl is the most harmless zombie poodle you'll ever meet.

Marceline's Bedroom

Every teenage girl needs an awesome bedroom, and Marceline is no exception—even if she's a thousand years old. Marceline's bedroom is exceptionally awesome. It's a place where she can rock out on her bass guitar. She plays her music a lot in there and even records her own albums. It has a full recording studio!

Throughout her house, including in her bedroom, Marceline has a lot of religious imagery from before the Mushroom War. On her bedroom walls, she has mounted several dead animal heads. They are a little creepy, but if you visit her house on your trip, they're definitely worth checking out.

Also, be sure to notice her closet. It's giant. A teen girl's dream.

Undead Gardener/ Garden/Plants

There is almost no plant life any of the Land of Ooo's kingdoms. But for some reason, it can be found at Marceline's house. This somehow-surviving plant life makes Marceline's house a great stop on a trip through the Land of Ooo. Make sure you take a picture because it will be the only vegetation you will see.

Marceline has an undead gardener who tends the grounds and maintains the gardens. Is it weird that a zombie keeps plants alive? Yes. Is it weirder than other stuff in the Land of Ooo? Not really. Especially if you think about how the gardener was probably alive before the Mushroom War and knew how to keep plants alive back then.

Important/ Historical Events

Marceline's house has been the site of some significant events, such as:

- The time she kicked Finn and Jake out of their Tree Fort, and they tried living in her house instead

- When it was the base of operations to combat Marceline's dad after Finn accidentally released him

- The time when Marceline and Jake helped prep Finn to ask Princess Bubblegum on a date

- The incident known as "Marceline's closet," when Finn and Jake went to the house to jam but got trapped in her closet

Marceline's Dad

Marceline and her dad, Hunson Abadeer, do not get along. At all. He is the ruler of the Nightosphere. His relationship with Marceline fell apart when he ate her fries at a broken-down diner many years ago. He claims to be pure evil, much like the Flame King and the Ice King. And he feels that eating his daughter's fries proves his evilness.

In addition to stealing fries, he also steals souls from people he meets. If you see him on your trip to the Land of Ooo, it's probably better if you turn and walk away as fast as you can. Like his daughter, he can shape-shift, fly, and change his size (among other über-creepy powers).

Nightosphere

Like the Fire Kingdom, the Nightosphere is a fiery pit of death and despair that we must warn against visiting. Unlike the Fire Kingdom, however, the Nightosphere is not actually in the Land of Ooo. It is in another dimension where the souls of the evil dead reside and do the bidding of their master, Hunson Abadeer. These dead souls are trapped in this dimension because Hunson captured them. Don't let him get you, too.

At times, there has been a portal between the Land of Ooo and the Nightosphere in Marceline's house. There's a portal back to the Land of Ooo in Hunson's home, but accessing it is nearly impossible given the legion of evil guards that protect it.

Cloud Kingdom

Looking for something fun to do at night during your trip to the Land of Ooo? Then make sure you visit the Cloud Kingdom. With everything made out of fluffy clouds, the Cloud Kingdom is renowned throughout all the other kingdoms as the place to go for wild parties and fun times. Everyone and everything in the Cloud Kingdom is all about partying. And after a long day of sightseeing, admit it—you'll want to relax and cut loose.

In the Cloud Kingdom, the Party God throws the best parties. He's a good person to meet and get in good with. If he likes you, he'll grant you a wish, and really—who doesn't want that?

Important/ Historical Events

Because the Cloud Kingdom is a party land, not too much of historical significance has occurred there. However, Finn and Jake have traveled there a couple of times, including:

- When Marceline kicked them out of their Tree Fort, they went to the Cloud Kingdom looking for a new place to live. They encountered a mean couple who wouldn't let them live in their cloud house.

- Jake went there one time after blacking out from laughing too hard at his own joke. He danced with

nymphs and met the Party God. Unfortunately, this all happened when he was supposed to be rescuing Finn. Jake got it together in time, though, and totally rescued his friend—after partying like a wild man!

Inside a large bush is the Wildberry
Kingdom. It's a hidden kingdom that
perhaps you'll miss if you don't look
really hard for it. It's in the middle of a
deep, deep valley in the middle of the
Land of Ooo. The creatures who live
there look like different kinds of berries.
They look delicious. As with the Candy
People, it's advised that one not eat the
citizens of the Wildberry Kingdom.

The Wildberry Kingdom is ruled by
the Wildberry Princess. She is beloved
by her people and even has her own
line of juices. (Don't think too hard

about that.) She looks like a Wildberry, but some of her outer berries fall off sometimes. When that happens, she needs to be taken to the hospital, as it is a life-threatening condition.

Important/ Historical Events

Most of the important events that have occurred in the Wildberry Kingdom have centered on the Wildberry Princess:

⚙ The Ice King has captured the Wildberry Princess on several occasions, but she's been rescued by Finn and Jake. She doesn't hate or fear the Ice King like most of the other princesses seem to. She doesn't love him, but she accepts him for what he is.

⚙ The Wildberry Princess was once the target of the deadly assassin Me-Mow. Jake was able to protect her from the murderous creature, allowing

her to continue ruling over
her people in their hidden bush
kingdom.

Evil Forest

On the outer edges of the Land of Ooo lies the Evil Forest. It is a spooky wood where dark creatures "live." We say "live" because it doesn't seem that anyone is actually "alive" as we understand it. Mostly they were once alive and are now zombies and monsters.

While the Evil Forest is full of the undead, it's not as perilous as you might imagine. It's scary, sure, but not totally dangerous. We don't have a travel restriction in place for the Evil Forest. Just make sure you're a brave adventurer.

In the Evil Forest, you'll find the crystal gem apple, which is a portal to the Crystal Kingdom. If you want to visit the Crystal Kingdom, a visit to the Evil Forest is required.

The undead creatures in the Evil Forest include dead trees that are gnarled and twisted into grotesque forms. They are among the elements that make the forest exceptionally scary. But they are basically harmless.

You can also see Skeleton Butterflies, which look just like you'd imagine. They're cute and, again, harmless, even if they look a little scary.

Then there are the Sign Zombies. They look like street signs of various types (STOP signs, WRONG WAY signs, etc.) come to life as zombies. Rather than give directions, these signs are evil and mean.

If you travel to the Evil Forest and encounter these forms of undead life, it's okay to look at them. You might be able to even have a picnic with them. But understand that they are scary. They may not hurt you, but they won't be too nice. Just be brave and smart as you interact with them.

Brain Beast

While most of the creatures in the Evil Forest are scary but mostly harmless, there are some that will mess you up if you encounter them. One of them is the Brain Beast, a floating mass of snakes that looks like a brain. In its center, it has a ruby from which it gets its power. The ruby is also the Brain Beast's point of weakness. If you see it in the Evil Forest, turn and run away — fast. If you can't run away fast enough, try to find a weapon to smash the ruby with. That will kill the creature before it kills you.

You may not encounter the creature. It's not known how many of them there are. Maybe there was just the one that Jake and Finn killed.

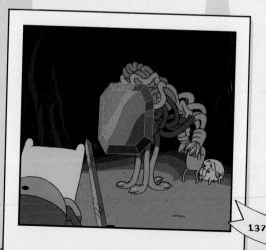

137

Wall of Flesh

Perhaps the creepiest, grossest creature in all of the Land of Ooo is the Wall of Flesh. It's a boneless mass of skin that lives in the Evil Forest. It will seemingly rise up from the ground and get in the way of travelers in the forest, stopping their progress. The creature known as Tree Trunks encountered the Wall of Flesh and thought he looked sad, so she covered it in stickers. The Wall of Flesh tried to eat Tree Trunks. Finn and Jake also battled the wall on that occasion, cutting off its arm. The wall retreated into some trees. It's believed that the wall lives in the undead trees of the Evil Forest.

As with most creatures in the Evil Forest, it's scary but not necessarily deadly. Also, it's supergross.

Important/ Historical Events

The Evil Forest has only been the scene of important or historical events a couple of times:

* There was the time that Tree Trunks went to the forest in search of the crystal gem apple. She encountered lots of the undead creatures along the way, having good experiences with some of them (such as

the Skeleton Butterflies), but bad experiences with others (like the Wall of Flesh and the Sign Zombies). If it weren't for adventurers Finn and Jake battling back the evil creatures of the Evil Forest, Tree Trunks may not have survived the Evil Forest.

⚙ Pretty much that's the most important event in the history of the Evil Forest. But if you're brave, you can create your own historical events!

Bad Lands/Desert Lands/Government

The areas known as the Bad Lands and the Desert Lands border each other. They are both relatively small areas in the Land of Ooo, and it's recommended that they be avoided by visitors. The Bad Lands are known primarily as the home of the Congressional Hall of the Land of Ooo (see page 144).

Neither of these border lands have any full-time residents. Their

environments are too harsh for anyone to live in.

The Desert Lands are essentially a graveyard. Lots of skeletons, broken ships, and weapons are visible there. It's thought to be the final resting place of much of the destruction from the Mushroom War.

Neither place is really worth visiting, unless you have a sick interest in death. Or government.

Royal Congressional Hall

In the Bad Lands, you'll find the Royal Tart Path. It is the safest, most protected road in all of the Land of Ooo as it leads directly to the Royal Congressional Hall. It's not available for public travel, however, as its primary purpose is the delivery of supplies for certain government ceremonies that take place in the Royal Congressional Hall.

The Royal Congressional Hall is the place where leaders of all the kingdoms meet every 150 years to participate in several ceremonies and determine the laws that will take effect throughout the land. If you're interested in a lot of really boring political stuff, then it might be worth a visit. If not, then don't worry about going there. There's a lot of way cooler stuff to see in the Land of Ooo.

Governments in the Land of Ooo

The Land of Ooo is divided into lots of kingdoms, as you know. These kingdoms are all ruled over by a king, queen, princess, duke, etc. That means their governments are called "monarchies." The challenge with having a monarchy is that one leader has all the power. This is great if you have a wonderful ruler like Princess Bubblegum, but if your ruler is evil, like the Ice King, it's terrible.

Each monarch is really focused on their own kingdom's needs and doesn't interact with the other monarchs very often. The kingdoms don't battle each other very much, or anything like that. There is thought to be some trade between the kingdoms. This is pretty rare, though, because who wants to trade candy for ice? Seriously.

Important Ceremonies

There are two important ceremonies that take place in the Royal Congressional Hall. They are each unique and have a great impact on the Land of Ooo.

The Grand Meeting of Ooo Royalty: This important meeting occurs once every 150 years, and it allows the rulers of each kingdom to get together to discuss the needs of Land of Ooo for the next 150 years.

The Backrub Ceremony: One of the most sacred events in all the Land of Ooo, several back-rubbers get together and rub the backs of the rulers and others who wish to attend. Royal tarts are served exclusively. If you're in town during these festivities, make it a point to be there, because who doesn't love a back rub and a royal tart?

Astral Plane

A strange dimension, the Astral Plane is a place where everyone's supernatural "astral self" resides. Finn found the Astral Plane while having an out-of-body experience after being frozen by the Ice King. There, Finn had a cool glowing body and could float around. Everything was peaceful and seemed to help Finn realize his truer self.

We've included it in this travel guide because it's a special place, but unfortunately we don't know how to help you see it or visit there. But if you do stumble upon it, beware of the Astral Beast.

Underworld

What happens when we die? That question has been asked for millions of years. Pretty much nobody knows. But in the Land of Ooo, we have an answer. When a creature dies, it goes to the Underworld, also known as the Land of the Dead.

The living (like you!) can visit the Underworld by staring cross-eyed at the corner of a wall in a building in the Land of Ooo.

If you go there, DO NOT DRINK FROM THE RIVER OF FORGETFULNESS. You'll lose all your memories.

You can also leave the Underworld by taking a giant escalator back to the world of the living. You'll have to prove to the guards you're alive, but that should be easy.

Be sure to get your picture taken in front of Death's Castle while you're there, because, why not?

Forest

When you were a kid, did your mom tell you fairy tales that took place in magical forests? Well, in the Land of Ooo, that kind of forest is real! Its location is a bit of a mystery, but Finn has found it. He traveled there to find a story to tell Jake when he was sick.

Living in the forest is a variety of talking animals like a Momma Bear and some talking ants. If you visit with these special magical animals, they will give you a story to tell your friends about your trip to the Land of Ooo.

So look for the forest on the map and make an effort to find it. You won't regret it!

Goblin Kingdom

The Goblin Kingdom is a smaller kingdom in the Land of Ooo. It's the home of the goblins (duh). If you want to meet goblins, you should go there. That's about the only reason to go. But there's a danger in visiting the Goblin Kingdom, and that is that they might try to make you their king. That sounds awesome, but it's really not. Sure, being a king gives you a lot of power, but King of the Goblins? Really?

Goblins are pretty much weak sauce. Jake and Finn beat them by clapping their hands in a rhythm. If that's all it takes, do you really want to be their king? Not even Finn wanted the job.

Multiverse

The idea behind the Multiverse is that there are countless parallel dimensions or universes similar to our own, but different in their own ways. Several Lands of Ooo exist in the Multiverse, similar to the main Land of Ooo, but slightly (or very) different. There's the Land of Ooo where everyone's genders are reversed, one where the Lich wished he never existed, and tons more.

You can go to the different dimensions by visiting the Time Room, which exists outside of time, in the center of the universe. There, you can pick the door to the universe you want to visit. You should give it a try. It's pretty wacky! Just be sure you know the way back to your home universe!

Conclusion

Oh, good, you survived to the end of the book. You are now ready to travel to the Land of Ooo. Make sure you take us along with you when you go on your next vacation to the Candy Kingdom or if you visit the Ice Kingdom. We'll help you find the way to where you want to go. And how to get back!